Have you read these Super Soccer Boy books?

Super Soccer Boy
and the Exploding Footballs

Super Soccer Boy
and the Evil Electronic Bunnies

Super Soccer Boy
and the Snot Monsters

Super Soccer Boy
and the Attack of the Giant Slugs

Super Soccer Boy
and the Alien Invasion

Coming Soon:

Super Soccer Boy
and the Raging Robots

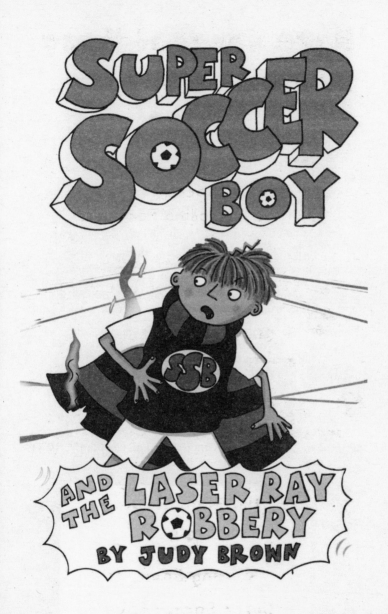

SUPER SOCCER BOY

AND THE LASER RAY ROBBERY

BY JUDY BROWN

Piccadilly Press • London

For Coco

First published in Great Britain in 2011 by
Piccadilly Press Ltd, 5 Castle Road, London NW1 8PR
www.piccadillypress.co.uk

Text and illustration copyright © Judy Brown, 2011

ISBN: 978 1 84812 150 8

1 3 5 7 9 10 8 6 4 2

Printed and bound by CPI Group (UK) Ltd, Croydon, CR0 4YY
Cover design by Simon Davis
Cover illustration by Judy Brown

Chapter One

School Trip Tedium

'Hurry up, Harry. You'll be late!' called Mum. This was the third time she had called him and she was beginning to get rather annoyed. 'HARRY!'

'Coming,' he called back and zoomed out of the kitchen, his pet rat, Ron, on his shoulder.

'Get a move on, Harry. You have to get to school or the coach for the museum trip will leave without you.'

'Booooring!' groaned Harry.

'Nonsense,' said Mum. 'You like Egyptian stuff.'

'Not as much as football,' he said.

'Yes, I'm well aware of that,' sighed Mum.

Harry had always been obsessed with football and ever since the weird flash of lightning that had transformed him from a useless footballer into Super Soccer Boy, his obsession had grown even stronger.

'Here's your lunch, Harry. Have a good day.'

'Thanks, Mum,' said Harry.

On the corner of Crumbly Drive, waiting patiently as usual, stood Jake, Harry's best friend.

'Morning, Harry. Ready for the trip?'

'S'pose so. Hope it's not too boring,' Harry grumbled.

'At least we get a day off lessons,' said Jake.

'But we'll have those stupid sheets to fill in, AND it means we'll miss football in PE.'

'Yeah, and tomorrow we'll all have to write a report about it in literacy. *My day at the museum* or something,' said Jake.

By the time they got to school, both Year Six classes were lined up in the playground and Miss Ford was taking the register.

'Hurry up, boys,' she said when she saw Harry and Jake. 'It's almost time to go.'

After registration, everyone piled on the coach. There was the usual bundle to get the back seats. Harry managed to weave through the other children with all the skill and speed he used when he was avoiding defenders and heading towards goal, and managed to bag the seats for Jake and his other friends.

Miss Ford and Mr Jenkins got on last and Miss Ford walked up and down the coach handing out pieces of paper to everyone.

'OK, listen up,' she said. 'It's only a short trip to Middletown Museum, but I want you all to look out of the windows on the way and mark off on these sheets as many of the landmarks as you can —'

Harry nudged Jake. 'Told you so.'

'When we arrive, I'll hand out sheets to fill in about the Egyptian exhibits. We'll have a guided tour of the exhibition and after that I want you to take notes and draw some pictures to use in your written work tomorrow.'

Everybody groaned.

Mr Jenkins stood up. 'We're very lucky to have an opportunity to see these wonderful artefacts. It's very unusual for an exhibition of this importance to come to a little place like Middletown. The golden funeral mask is famous throughout the world, so for you to see it "in the flesh" so to speak will be a marvellous experience.'

'And,' added Miss Ford, 'the curator has worked very hard to bring such an important exhibition to our museum, so I hope you'll show a bit more enthusiasm when we get there. Remember, no eating on the coach and keep the noise to a dull roar if you can.'

And with that the coach set off.

Chapter Two

Exhibition Excitement

Twenty minutes later, on the other side of Middletown, the coach arrived at the museum.

'Remember, everyone,' said Mr Jenkins as they got off the coach, 'best behaviour at all times. Stay together and, above all, be sensible.'

There was a huge banner across the front of the museum. It read *Treasures of the Silver Pharaoh*. But that wasn't what Harry was staring at. On the wall by the entrance of the museum was a poster, which said *Coming Soon — World Cup Football Exhibition*.

'AWESOME!' said Harry.

'What?' asked Jake, surprised at his friend's sudden enthusiasm for things Egyptian. 'I thought you said it was going to be boring.'

'No, not *that*. Look!' said Harry. He pointed at the poster and beamed. 'The World Cup exhibition. It's coming here. Now that's one exhibition I *have* to go to.'

'Oh,' said Jake, not hugely interested. He wasn't quite as nuts about football as Harry, but then who was?

'Come on, kids, don't dawdle,' said Mr Jenkins.

The Year Sixes bundled into the museum to be greeted by a tall thin man with a large moustache. Miss Ford introduced him.

'Professor Niblett, the museum's curator, has kindly agreed to show us around the exhibition himself,' she said. 'So I hope you will all listen carefully to what he has to say.'

'Thank you, Miss Ford, and welcome, children, to Middletown Museum.' He smiled a greasy, unconvincing smile, and Harry took an immediate dislike to him.

Harry had found that since he'd become Super Soccer Boy, all his senses were now sharper and he noticed things about people that no one else did. If he thought someone seemed dodgy, they usually were.

'If you'd like to follow me, I will show you the treasures of Pharaoh Psusennes I, also known as the Silver Pharaoh.'

The Professor turned and strode into a room on his right. He reminded Harry of a praying mantis.

The children followed.

'What an annoying man,' Harry said to Jake as they walked around the exhibition listening to the curator.

'That's a bit harsh,' said Jake. 'He's just a bit old

and crusty. My mum says he was here when she was a kid.'

'There's something about him I don't like. He's got a creepy smile,' said Harry.

'Here we go again,' Jake muttered. He was used to Harry's sharp observations, even if it usually landed them in trouble.

The tour was actually very interesting. Like most people, the children were fascinated by the mummies, although Millie and a couple of the more squeamish Year Sixes did feel a bit funny when Professor Niblett went into graphic details about pulling brains through nostrils during mummification.

The best thing, apart from the
room with the mummies, was
a magnificent sarcophagus
made from solid silver, and
the beautiful gold
funeral mask.

'Wow!'
said Harry.

In fact
they were all
pretty impressed.

'It's beauuutiful!'
said Chloe.

'That must be worth a
fortune,' said Will, gazing at it admiringly.

'The mask is, in fact, priceless, young man.
Irreplaceable. It is by far the most valuable item
in the collection and indeed, in the entire
museum,' said the Professor. 'It's made of solid
gold and so it is extremely heavy. It actually took
three people to place it in position. A wonderful

treasure indeed,' he added dreamily. 'As you can imagine, it has to be very well protected which is why we have security cameras on it at all times, day and night.'

Afterwards, they divided into pairs and went around the museum filling in their sheets.

'Is it lunchtime yet?' asked Jake. 'I'm starving.'

'As usual,' said Harry.

'Ten minutes till lunch,' said Miss Ford quietly as she came up behind them. 'Pass it on to anyone else you see. Meet in the foyer and then we'll eat our lunch in the courtyard.'

Jake's stomach rumbled.

Ten minutes later, most of the school party was waiting patiently in the foyer, eager to eat their packed lunches.

Just as Mr Jenkins arrived with the last few stragglers, the lights in the foyer flickered off and on, as if something was wrong with the electricity supply. Suddenly, there was an almighty ringing as all the museum alarms went off.

'The power surge must have set the alarm off,' said Jake.

Four guards dashed out of the security office and ran around like headless chickens. Three more ran into the foyer and surrounded the children.

'Or maybe not!' said Harry.

'Close the museum! Close the museum! We must have total shutdown!!' shouted the curator rushing down the corridor into the foyer.

'Perkins, search the museum!' he ordered.

'Yes, sir,' he said scuttling off.

'Benson, Robson, check the exits!'

'Sir!' Off they went.

'You two, come with me. Barker, stay here with our – guests.'

The curator strode off on his long lanky legs with the guards trotting to keep up. Rushy Meadow Year Six stood in the foyer wondering what would happen next.

It didn't take long before they found out.

'Nooooooooo!' came a voice wailing through the corridors. 'Nooo! Not the mask! I don't believe it! It's impossible!'

The curator came charging back to the foyer.

'There's been a robbery!' he was shouting. 'The funeral mask – it's gone!'

Chapter Three

CSI:
Middletown

As soon as the alarm had sounded, large metal grilles had dropped down in front of the museum entrance. In the background, they could hear the sound of police sirens getting rapidly louder. It was quite scary, but very exciting.

Then the lights flickered again.

'What a calamity!' wailed the Professor, mopping his brow with a large hanky. 'What am I to do?'

'What's happened?' asked Mr Jenkins.

'The golden funeral mask!' said the Professor. 'It's been stolen!'

'Stolen?!' exclaimed Miss Ford. 'But how? How could anyone steal that great big, heavy thing in broad daylight?'

The children murmured amongst themselves.

'Did any of you see anything, Year Six?' asked Mr Jenkins.

'No, sir,' they all answered, nervously.

Outside the museum there was a screech of tyres and three police cars and a police van drew up. The curator ran over to release one of the metal grilles and a dozen policemen poured into the museum.

'Nobody move!' one of them shouted very dramatically.

Lauren burst into tears.

They were followed by two plain-clothed policemen, one of whom clearly thought he was something special.

'Who's in charge here?' he boomed and a couple more nervous Year Sixes began to cry. The rest of them couldn't wait to see what would happen next.

The curator introduced himself. 'That would be me, Professor Niblett, I am the curator, er . . .'

'Inspector Bird,' said the policeman. There was a definite snigger from amongst the group of children.

'Ahem,' said Inspector Bird. 'What seems to have occurred?'

'It's dreadful, Inspector,' said the Professor, looking as though he was going to faint. 'The golden funeral mask of Psusennes I seems to have been stolen from the museum.'

'And when was it last seen?' he asked.

'Well, it was here when I showed these

children around the exhibition this morning . . .
and now it's gone!' he wailed again.

Inspector Bird frowned hard at the group of
children in the museum foyer. Lauren began to
cry again.

'Now look, Inspector,' said Miss Ford
indignantly. 'I hope you're not suggesting that
one of my pupils has anything to do with this.
Have you actually *seen* the item in question? If
you had, I think you'd know that it is far too big
and heavy for any of them to have taken.'

'No, madam, but I'm afraid none of you can be allowed out of the museum until there has been a thorough search of the building and the people in it. And that includes the children.'

'This is exciting!' said Will. 'It's like an episode of *Crime Scene*.'

'No murders though,' said George, sounding a bit disappointed.

'Now if you would like to get the children in an orderly line behind yourself and your colleague, Sergeant Mills can start to take some names, addresses and witness statements.'

Harry glanced at the curator and was sure he detected a slight glint in his eye, as if he were enjoying the whole drama.

'OK, children,' said Mr Jenkins, 'line up just like we do in the playground.'

They all groaned.

'How long will this take, sir?' asked Kate. 'I've got drama club after school and we're trying on costumes today.'

'Inspector, how long will you need to keep us here?' asked Mr Jenkins. 'I'll have to notify the parents if we're not back by the end of school.'

'As long as it takes,' the Inspector replied sternly. 'This is a serious business.' And he turned and strode off after the curator.

Professor Niblett led the Inspector to the museum room that had, until very recently, housed the golden funeral mask. The Inspector inspected it, but found no clues. The crime scene team were photographing and fingerprinting everything in sight.

'So, Professor, how large was the item, would you say?'

'It was about a metre tall and made of solid gold,' replied the Professor.

'So it was heavy then?'

'*Very* heavy, Inspector. It took three people to put it in position.'

'And there are no workmen here today, nothing out of the ordinary?'

'Nothing,' agreed the Professor. 'Only the children as you have seen.'

The Inspector wandered around the room, poking about under stands and looking behind display boards, but he was mystified. 'Is that CCTV always on?' he asked, pointing up at a camera in the corner of the room.

'Of course, Inspector,' said the Professor. 'Always.'

'Well then, why are we wasting our time here? Let's go and see what it tells us,' he said and rubbed his hands together.

Chapter Four

Dodgy Electrics?

Back in the museum foyer, the children were getting restless.

'Can we eat, sir?' asked Jake. 'It's way past lunchtime now.'

'I suppose you may as well,' said Mr Jenkins.

'Looks like we're stuck here for a while. Just don't make too much mess.'

Harry watched as the Inspector followed the curator past the toilets and into a room labelled *Security Office*. He desperately wanted to hear what they were talking about.

'Please, sir, I need the loo,' Harry said to the teacher.

'Can't it wait, Harry?' said Mr Jenkins. 'I think it's best we all stay together.'

'Er, no, sir,' he winced. 'We had curry last night and —'

'OK, OK, spare us the gory details. Sergeant, is it all right for Harry to use the gents?'

'Yes, it's been searched already. But no hanging around, lad, OK?'

'Sure,' said Harry and dashed off.

Ever since he'd become Super Soccer Boy, Harry's hearing was so good that he could even hear what players were whispering at the far end of the pitch. He had decided to use this super skill to listen to what was going on behind the security door, but with the heavy door shut, he needed to be as close as possible.

Fortunately for Harry, next to the toilet was a large potted plant, just big enough for him to hide behind.

SECURITY OFFICE

'I don't know what could have happened, Inspector – it's always on normally,' said the curator.

'But you said there was some sort of a power surge before the alarm went off,' the Inspector said.

'Yes, the lights flickered. I was about to go and find the caretaker to see if we had an electrical problem when I saw that the mask was missing. Oh, it's a tragedy, a tragedy!' he whimpered.

'Yes, yes indeed. So after the power surge, why did some of the cameras switch off?'

'I've no idea – all that sort of thing is beyond me. I'm just a simple historian. I know nothing about technical things. Or science for that matter,' he said feebly.

'Interesting,' Harry said to himself. 'So someone switched off the cameras.'

'The fact is,' said the exasperated Inspector, 'there is no recording of

the incident, but the camera is working again now. One minute the mask is there, and the next minute, it's gone. It would be too heavy for one person to carry, and certainly too big to hide. But the only people who were in the museum this morning were all these schoolchildren and their teachers.'

'It would seem so,' said the curator.

The door began to open and Harry whooshed at super soccer speed back to the foyer.

'What was that?' said the curator as he came out of the office.

'What was what?' asked the Inspector.

'Oh, I just thought I saw someone, but it was nothing,' said the curator looking at the leaves on the museum floor.

It was another two hours before the police had finished with Year Six and they were allowed back on the coach. They had all been questioned, their names and addresses taken and they'd given statements that were pretty much the same. None of them were of any help to the police.

'You know that power surge,' Harry said to Jake, 'the one before the alarms went off?'

'What about it?' Jake asked.

'It switched off the power to some of the cameras, including the ones in the golden mask room. I heard the curator telling Inspector Bird.'

'What a name!' said Jake, laughing.

'A bit convenient, don't you think? That it included that particular camera going off,' Harry continued.

'I guess so,' said Jake.

'Makes me think it's an inside job,' said Harry.

He looked out of the coach window as it drew away.

Inspector Bird, Sergeant Mills and Professor Niblett were standing on the steps of the museum in deep conversation with the museum caretaker.

'I don't understand how anyone could get that great big thing out of the museum without being seen,' said Jake.

'Me neither,' said Harry. 'But I'm going to find out.'

Chapter Five

Naughty Niblett

When the Inspector had left the museum and all the staff had gone home, Professor Niblett picked up his briefcase and locked his office door, humming to himself.

'Goodnight, sir,' said the head security guard

as the Professor walked through the foyer. 'Don't worry, the police have left some of their men for extra security in case of any more, er . . . incidents.'

'Thank you, Barker,' he said seriously. 'See you in the morning.'

He walked down the steps of the museum, got into his Smart car, patted his jacket pocket and smiled to himself.

At home, Harry was stuffing himself with pizza and telling his mum and dad about the robbery. It had been on the news all day but it was really interesting to hear Harry's firsthand account.

'It was quite exciting really – all those police and sirens and stuff.'

'No clues as to how it was done, though?' asked Dad.

'Not so far I don't think.'

'It's terrible, stealing world treasures. So selfish. They should be for everyone,' said Mum crossly, clearing away the dinner plates.

'Someone'll probably melt it down for the gold if you ask me,' said Dad.

'I'm just going on the computer to look up some stuff about the pharaoh for school tomorrow,' said Harry, jumping up.

'Oh, OK,' said Mum. 'Don't stay on it for too long though – you know what you're like once you get started.'

Harry booted up the computer and went straight to Google, but instead of typing in *Pharaoh Psusennes I*, he typed in *Professor Niblett*, the curator of Middletown Museum.

Harry clicked on several of the results to read the articles and then he spotted a few that really caught his interest.

Golden statue snatched from centre of Brussels

Golden statue of the Madonna stolen in Milan

Golden Buddha stolen

He clicked on one of them.

A replica of the solid gold Buddha from the golden temple in Bangkok was stolen today. The statue was being exhibited in a museum in Rome. Several curators from European museums were attending a conference at the time. 'It's a tragedy,' said Professor Niblett of Middletown Museum in England . . .

'Hmm,' said Harry. 'I wonder if there were

museum conferences going on when the other things were stolen.'

There were. And Professor Niblett had been attending every single one.

'Gotcha!' said Harry to himself. 'But how on earth did you do it?'

In the comfortable mansion that had been in his family for years, Professor Niblett sat at his kitchen table with his dinner in front of him. He reached into his jacket pocket, took out a tiny golden funeral mask and placed it on the table in front of him.

His mind drifted as he stared at the tiny golden thing and began to eat his dinner.

40

HE KEPT IT LOCKED IN A ROOM IN THE BASEMENT OF THE FAMILY'S MANSION...

...A PLACE THAT NIGEL'S PARENTS NEVER BOTHERED TO GO.

AS HE GREW OLDER THOUGH, NIGEL WAS NO LONGER SATISFIED WITH LITTLE TRINKETS.

HE WANTED BIGGER THINGS...

...MORE MAGNIFICENT!

HE KNEW IT WOULD BE REALLY TRICKY. ANYTHING BIG WOULD BE MUCH TOO DIFFICULT TO HIDE...

THERE MUST BE A WAY!!

MIDDLETOWN NEWS

EXPLORERS LOST!

...AND WHEN HIS PARENTS WERE LOST ON AN EXPEDITION IN DARKEST PERU, LEAVING NIGEL THE MANSION ALL TO HIMSELF, HE VOWED HE WOULD FIND IT.

Smiling, Professor Niblett pushed away his plate and picked up his briefcase and the little golden mask.

'Let's take you down to your new home, and tomorrow you can join my lovely collection,' he said.

At 49 Crumbly Drive, Harry was on the phone to Jake.

'Are you busy after school tomorrow?' asked Harry.

'Not unless the police arrest me for stealing the funeral mask,' said Jake. 'Why – do you want to play football or something?'

'No, it's about the robbery. I think I know who did it,' said Harry. 'I just don't know how.'

Jake knew what was coming next. 'Don't tell me, we're going to be playing detective, aren't we?'

'How did you guess?' said Harry, laughing.

'Know you too well,' said Jake, already feeling nervous.

'See you tomorrow then,' said Harry. 'Night.'

'Night, Harry,' said Jake, wondering what he'd let himself in for this time.

Chapter Six

Niblett Mansion

Harry had a restless night. He dreamt that the museum curator had broken into their house and stolen all his football trophies. When he awoke, he saw Ron looking at him with a troubled expression.

'It's OK, Ron, just a bad dream,' he said and glanced over at his trophies, to make sure they were all still there.

After breakfast, Harry met Jake as usual on the way to school and told him what he'd found out on the internet.

'It doesn't mean he's the thief,' said Jake. 'It could just be a coincidence.'

'It *could* be, I suppose, but I'm pretty sure it's

not. I thought he seemed dodgy even before the funeral mask disappeared, remember? Anyway, if he's not the thief we'll be doing him a favour by proving him innocent!'

'And if he *is* the thief we'll probably end up in a heap of trouble,' grumbled Jake.

'It'll be fine!' Harry assured him. 'It always has been so far, hasn't it?'

'So far . . . I guess . . . just about,' said Jake, resigned to his fate.

'Anyway, I looked him up and he lives in Niblett Mansion,' said Harry. 'The bus stop's just round the corner and if we go there straight after school we can look around before he gets back from the museum.'

'Would it make any difference if I said it all seems a bit crazy?' asked Jake.

'Nah, not really,' said Harry and grinned. 'We should have loads of time before he gets back.

The museum shuts late on Fridays — about seven-thirty. They have special lectures. Mum goes sometimes. Great, here's the bus!'

So, that afternoon, Harry and Jake went home to change, and then they walked to the bus stop.

'I made sure my mobile is fully charged in case we need to call for help,' said Harry.

'Very reassuring,' said Jake sarcastically.

'And I brought some food, just in case — as long as Ron doesn't eat it all before we get the chance.'

He looked in his backpack to make sure that Ron hadn't got the lid off his lunchbox. His favourite football was in there too — he never went anywhere without it.

'Exactly how long do you think this is going to take?' Jake asked, alarmed.

'No idea,' said Harry.

Professor Niblett had spent half the day on the phone talking to the press, the insurance company and the Egyptian Embassy. A large group of press from all over the world had set up camp outside the museum.

There was a knock on the door and Inspector Bird came in.

'Good afternoon, Inspector. Any luck?'

'None whatsoever, I'm afraid. We have found absolutely nothing out of the ordinary, apart from the security camera glitch. An electrician's coming in to thoroughly check the wiring so I'll need you to close the museum early today.'

'What about the evening lecture!' said the Professor. 'It's due to start at five-thirty. It's about Byzantine Art of the Middle Ages, a fascinating —'

'Not today, I'm afraid. The museum will be off limits while the electrical system is being tested. The building needs to be cleared by six.'

'Very well, Inspector,' sighed the Professor. 'I'll have the staff put some signs up to inform the public and put a notification on our website.'

'Thank you, Professor,' said the Inspector, and left the office.

'That actually works out rather well,' Professor Niblett said to himself. He leant back in his chair and closed his eyes, thinking back to the day he first had his brilliant idea.

ONE DAY

WHEN HE WAS AT UNIVERSITY, STUDYING FOR A DEGREE IN MOLECULAR SCIENCE...

...NIGEL NIBLETT HAD A BRILLIANT IDEA

WHAT IF HE COULD MAKE THINGS SMALLER!!!

IF HE COULD SHRINK THINGS UNTIL THEY WERE SMALL ENOUGH TO FIT IN HIS POCKET.

WHEN HE FINISHED HIS DEGREE, HE STAYED ON AT THE UNIVERSITY AND STUDIED ARCHAEOLOGY. HE KNEW SO MUCH ABOUT IT ALREADY, THAT IT GAVE HIM TIME TO EXPERIMENT ON MAKING THINGS REALLY TINY.

IT WASN'T LONG BEFORE HE REALISED THAT LASERS WERE THE ANSWER...

52

...AND AFTER YEARS OF WORK, HE FINALLY SUCCEEDED IN DEVELOPING A SHRINKING AND ENLARGING **RAY!**

AFTER BECOMING A PROFESSOR, NIGEL APPLIED FOR A JOB AS CURATOR OF THE MUSEUM IN HIS HOME TOWN OF MIDDLETOWN.

BEING A CURATOR, GAVE PROFESSOR

NIBLETT ACCESS TO MUSEUMS ALL OVER THE **WORLD!!**

NOW HIS COLLECTION

LOVELY!

WOULD KNOW NO BOUNDS

53

The ringing phone brought Professor Niblett out of his daydream.

'Middletown Museum, Professor Niblett speaking,' he said.

'Good afternoon,' said a voice. 'I am Felicity Philips from the *Middletown Echo* and I wondered —'

'No more statements!' said the Professor, and slammed down the phone. He was sick of talking to reporters and suddenly he couldn't wait to get home.

Chapter Seven

Magnificent Magnifying Machine

At that very moment, Harry and Jake got off the bus and walked round the corner to the grand entrance of Niblett Mansion.

Jake looked down the driveway. 'There's a security camera,' he said. 'On the big porch thing over the door.'

'I see it,' said Harry. 'Not a problem.'

He got his football out of his backpack and placed it on the driveway. 'Just need to redirect it a bit.'

With Super Soccer Boy accuracy, Harry booted the football straight at the camera, knocking it upwards, so that all it was filming were the fluffy white clouds floating along in the sky.

'Neat,' said Jake.

'Come on, let's find a way in,' said Harry, and set off down the path.

Harry collected his football and they did a circuit of the house looking for open windows. There was one, but it was on the top floor, and only open a crack.

'We can't get in. That's it, then,' said Jake hopefully – although he didn't really believe it was.

'It's OK, I brought my Utility Boots just in case.' Harry stopped and took out the special football boots he had designed and built himself to enhance his Super Soccer powers. He put them on and pressed the button that said *Hover*

on his remote control, gently rising off the ground towards a partly open window on the second floor. It was too small a gap for him to squeeze through, but Ron scampered in easily enough. He seemed to understand the problem and helped open the window from the inside.

'I'm in!' Harry said a few seconds later, and clambered through the window.

You don't say? thought Jake.

A couple of minutes later, Jake saw one of the downstairs windows open.

'Jake, quick, climb in here!' called Harry.

Jake ran over and climbed in.

'Wow! This place looks even bigger on the inside!' said Jake. 'Why on earth would someone with so much cash bother to steal things?'

'I don't think it's about the money,' said Harry. 'Let's look around.'

It seemed the Professor lived alone. They had a quick search of the house and Harry saw nothing suspicious – until they reached the kitchen. On the table was a copy of *New Scientist* and that's when Harry realised he'd seen a whole shelf full of them in the study.

'That's odd,' he said, pointing at the magazine.

'What is?' asked Jake. 'It's just a boring science magazine, there's nothing here.'

'Yes, but Professor Niblett told the Inspector that he didn't know anything about science. Why would he be reading *New Scientist* unless he was interested in science?'

'Beats me,' said Jake. 'Maybe he's keen on learning new things. You know what adults are like.'

Harry spotted the door to the cellar. 'I wonder what's down there,' he said.

Harry found the light switch and started downstairs.

'Not interested in science, huh?' said Harry when he got to the bottom and looked around.

'Wow!' said Jake. 'It's a total lab. I wonder what he does down here.'

They had just started to search the place when suddenly there was a crunching noise from

outside and they both looked up at the small basement window.

'What was that?!' whispered Jake.

'Sounded like a car pulling up to me.'

Sure enough, the next thing they heard was the opening and closing of a car door, footsteps on the gravel, and a key turning in the front door of the mansion.

'Oh . . . my . . . God!' said Jake. 'He's back! What do we do now? I thought you said the museum closes at seven-thirty – it's only just gone six!'

'Must be something to do with the robbery. Quick – HIDE!' Harry whispered.

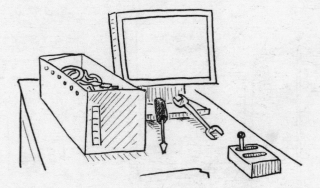

There was a hurried scramble as Jake dived into a big empty box in the corner and Harry squeezed himself under the lab bench at the side of the room.

'Tra la la la la,' sang the Professor happily as he entered the kitchen. 'La la . . . What's this?' he said out loud. 'I don't remember leaving the light on.'

Harry and Jake froze.

The Professor laughed. 'Ha! I must be getting old.' He trotted down the stairs to his basement lab, and Harry remembered to pull his rucksack out of sight just in time.

From under the bench, Harry looked around him. At the far end of the room, he could see a

large plinth, and there, with the super soccer eyesight that meant he could see a player's slightest movement from the other end of the pitch, Harry spotted a little gold statue sitting on it. It reminded him of something, but he wasn't sure what it was.

Professor Niblett walked over to the tiny statue, picked it up and polished it on his jacket.

'Nice and shiny, that's what we want. Nice and shiny!' he said.

He stepped back a few paces, opened a big shiny case and took something out. It looked a bit like a laser gun from a science fiction film.

The Professor placed it on a stand in front of the plinth and grinned. Harry was watching every move, fascinated, and so was Jake from a little hole in the box.

Professor Niblett pressed a few buttons and took a small device out of his briefcase. He put the device into the laser gun.

'Here we go!' said the Professor, pushing a lever forward.

A brilliant beam of light was directed at the tiny statue and, to Harry and Jake's amazement, it began to grow, very slowly at first, then faster and faster, until it was about a metre high!

Harry realised now what it had reminded him of – the funeral mask at the museum. In fact, he realised, it really *was* the funeral mask! He had to try really hard not to gasp.

Then the beam shut off.

So that's how he did it! thought Harry. *The little device shrinks things, and to blow them back up, you put the device in the laser gun. Neat!*

Jake was also thinking that he'd found a very dusty box to hide in and that his nose had begun to tickle.

'Beautiful! I am such a genius. Mwahaha-hahaha!' said Professor Niblett. He went over and released a lever on the side of the plinth and four wheels popped out underneath. 'And now to add you to the rest of my collection.'

He pushed the plinth towards the wall at the end of the room and punched in a series of numbers on a security panel. The entire back wall of the basement began to sink into the floor.

When he saw what was behind it, Harry couldn't believe his eyes.

Chapter Eight

Lost and Found

As the wall disappeared, amazing treasures were revealed. It was as if they were suddenly in the museum itself. There were paintings, sculptures, artefacts – some that Harry was sure he'd seen in books at school. And then Harry almost screamed in anguish as he saw something very familiar – it was the original gold World Cup trophy! Known as the Jules Rimet trophy, it had already been stolen once, in 1966, but was found by a little dog. Then it was stolen in 1983 in Rio de Janeiro, and had never been seen again. Everyone assumed it had been melted down. Obviously not!

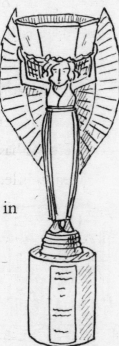

The fiend! thought Harry, almost bursting with anger. *How dare he steal it and keep it for himself. He must have been doing this for years.*

Professor Niblett pushed the plinth into his secret museum and transferred it onto a stand between the Jules Rimet trophy and the armour of a Samurai warrior.

'There,' he said. 'Lovely.' He stepped back and

admired his collection. 'Hmmm. It's getting a bit full in here. I'm going to need another room. I suppose I could shrink you all down to fit but it simply wouldn't be the same. But now, my lovelies, it's time for my dinner. All this excitement has made me rather hungry!'

Meanwhile, in the dusty box, Jake was watching with such amazement that he'd forgotten how much his nose was tickling and that he was supposed to stay super quiet.

'*AAAAACHOOOO!*' sneezed Jake.

'What was that?' said the Professor swinging around to look in the direction of the unexpected sneeze. He could see that the box in the corner of the lab was quivering. 'COME OUT OF THERE!' demanded Professor Niblett. 'WHOEVER YOU ARE!'

Then the box really started to shake.

'Leg it, Jake!' shouted Harry, emerging from under the bench. He knew that with his super

soccer speed, he'd easily be able to escape, but he couldn't leave Jake behind.

Jake half stumbled, half fell out of the box and Harry ran over to help him up.

'Run!' Harry said, but his backpack caught round the end of the banisters and pulled him back.

'Oh no, you don't!' yelled Professor Niblett. Quite speedily for a man of his age, he darted over to the laser ray gun, snatched out the device he'd put in it a short time before, and pointed it at Harry and Jake. 'You won't get away from me!' he snarled and pressed the button in the middle.

In an instant, Harry and Jake were shrunk to the size of a referee's whistle! They stood there looking at each other, totally stunned by what had just happened. Then two giant hands lifted them off the ground.

'He he he he!' said Professor Niblett. 'Don't you look hilarious? He he he he!'

Harry and Jake were not at all amused, and Jake for one was terrified.

'Put us down!' shouted Harry, kicking and struggling, but at his current size even his super soccer skills weren't going to be much help.

'He he he, that tickles!' said the Professor. 'Stop it or I'll squeeze . . . Hey wait a minute – I've seen you before. You were on the school trip yesterday. Is that why you're snooping around here?'

'You've got the old World Cup in there, you thief!' shouted Harry, but his voice came out all squeaky.

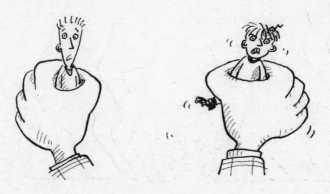

'Yes, I have! Isn't it nice and shiny and golden? I do so love shiny, precious things.' He paused and looked more serious. 'Now then, what am I to do with you? This is rather a nuisance.' He was beginning to realise what a difficult situation he had suddenly found himself in.

'This is going to take some thinking about. I will have to alter my plans slightly. I need to make a list!' he decided. 'Can't do that on an empty stomach, though. In fact, I think I'll sleep on it.'

Professor Niblett carried Harry and Jake into his secret museum and dropped them into the Jules Rimet trophy.

'There, you can have a really close look at it while I think of somewhere better to put you.'

Harry looked around him and thought of all the famous footballers that had held the cup – the cup that they were now trapped in! He'd always wanted to be in the World Cup – but this wasn't what he'd had in mind!

The Professor wheeled the now empty plinth back into its place in the lab and began to look for a container to put the boys in.

He found a pouring beaker. 'Aha, this will do. Don't want you to suffocate do we – that wouldn't be very pleasant.' The beaker had a rubber bung, which had enough of a gap around it to let air in but not to let Harry and Jake out. Then he lifted them from the World Cup and popped them inside. The Professor picked up Harry's backpack and chucked it in the room before closing the wall panel.

'Bye, bye, boys. See you in the morning,' he said.

Chapter Nine

A Tiny Bit of a Problem

'Now, what are we going to do?' said Jake, dejectedly, dropping to his knees.

'We have to get out of here, of course,' said Harry, trying to sound cheerful.

'And how are we supposed to do that? Look

at us — we're human shrimps!'

'Maybe I can use the power of my Utility Boots?' suggested Harry. He turned them on to their jet power setting and aimed himself at the rubber bung, but he just kept bumping his head against it and bouncing off. He soon stopped trying.

'It looks like we're stuck here overnight,' said Harry rubbing his head miserably.

'And then some,' said Jake. 'Our mums'll be frantic.'

'Good point,' said Harry, getting worried himself. 'Wait though, we still have our phones. If they work when they're this tiny.' Harry dug his out of his pocket and looked at it. 'Good, there's still a signal. We can let them know we're OK, but we won't tell them the trouble we're in until we really need to. I don't want to risk being grounded during the footie season!'

'But they'll know something's wrong when they hear our squeaky voices,' said Jake.

'We can text then!' said Harry. 'I'll text my mum and ask if I can stay at yours tonight, and you can text your mum and ask to stay at mine.'

A few moments later, their phones both played a high-pitched version of their *message sent* tones, and they were both very relieved.

'What if our mums say no?' Jake wondered.

'We'll just have to hope they don't, I guess,' said Harry. 'But it's Saturday tomorrow – so I don't see why they'd mind.'

Fortunately, both sets of parents were so used to having the boys stay over that they texted back quickly saying it was fine. That problem sorted, Harry and Jake sat down to work out their next move.

Jake's stomach rumbled.

'I can't believe you're hungry now,' Harry said laughing. 'Wait! God, I'm stupid! Ron is still in the backpack! He didn't get shrunk like we did!'

They both jumped up to see where Professor Niblett had chucked the backpack.

'Look, over there, right by the golden Buddha. We have to attract his attention,' said Harry. 'Shout as loud as you can and bang on the glass.'

It didn't seem to be working and they were growing hoarse.

'How can we make more noise?' said Jake. 'He can't hear us.'

'Let's try the mobiles. Turn them up really loud and play ring tones or something.'

Inside the backpack, Ron was wondering what was going on. A little while ago he'd been flying through the air and he'd landed with a thump. He was waiting for Harry to check he was OK,

but he couldn't even hear his voice any more. He wasn't particularly keen to come out on his own though, because he'd heard some shouting and there had been some sort of weird light so bright that he'd even been able to see it through the backpack. Best just to wait and listen for Harry . . . but he still couldn't hear him.

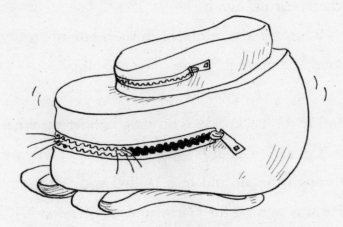

He could hear something though. What was it? It was high pitched and squeaky, but somehow familiar. It was time to get out and have a look.

'It's working!' said Harry. 'Look, the bag's moving.'

Ron's nose popped out and his whiskers twitched.

'Keep up the noise!'

With a rat's keen sense of hearing, Ron could hear the tiny mobile's tiny sounds. He poked his whole head out and looked around. He was in a room filled with big yellow shiny objects, but there was no sign of Harry. The shouty man was gone though so he decided to come out.

'There he is!' said Jake. 'Ron! RON!! RON!!! Over here!' he yelled as loudly as he possibly could.

Ron listened hard. He could hear a faint noise

and looked over in the direction it was coming from. That's when he finally spotted Harry, although he looked rather different now. Rather . . . smaller.

'He's coming!' said Harry as Ron started to scamper over. He ran to the side of the display stand and appeared in front of the glass beaker. It was a big shock. Ron was almost ten times taller than they were. It was actually quite scary.

'I'm glad he's on our side,' said Jake, with a wobble in his voice.

'Me too,' said Harry, gulping. Harry pointed at the bung in the beaker and made a pushing motion, hoping Ron would understand.

Fortunately for Harry and Jake, Ron was a very clever rat. Ron pushed the beaker onto its side and started nibbling and clawing at the bung and it wasn't long before it came loose.

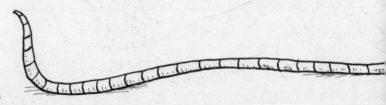

Harry and Jake ran out and hugged Ron gratefully.

Harry stopped for a moment and gazed up at the Jules Rimet trophy.

'It's magnificent, isn't it?' he said dreamily.

'Yes, it's lovely, Harry, but we have other things to think about right now,' said Jake. 'I mean we're out of *there*, but how do we get out of *here*?'

'I'm thinking about that, don't worry,' Harry replied. 'Let's get down anyway.'

They climbed onto Ron's back and he took them down to the floor.

'Well, how about something to eat?' said Jake. 'We're stuck here all night and there's a giant sandwich in your backpack.'

Harry laughed.

It took all three of them to open the lunchbox. Harry and Jake sat on the edge and nibbled on bits of sandwich while Ron chomped away happily.

'We need to get back to full size,' said Harry.

'You don't say!' Jake said, struggling with a giant biscuit.

'So we need to get hold of that thing the Prof used to shrink us. We have to get it and put it in the laser gun and do exactly what he did.'

'Sounds easy when you say it,' Jake told him.

'I have an idea of what we can do, with Ron's

help.' Harry yawned. 'But I'm really tired. Let's get some sleep. I'll set the alarm on my phone because I'll need to get up early to get things set up before the Prof comes back.'

Ron was already asleep – he was full of sausage and tomato sauce sandwich. Harry jumped down from the lunchbox and snuggled into Ron's fur to keep warm.

'That looks cosy,' said Jake, jumping down to join them.

Minutes later they were both asleep too.

Chapter Ten

A Large
Improvement

They slept surprisingly well and it was Harry's
phone alarm that woke them.

'So what's the plan?' asked Jake, stretching.

'Well, the Prof's not seen Ron, so I'll make
him think that we've been eaten by a rat.'

'Sweet!' giggled Jake.

'We'll spread some of the tomato sauce from the sandwich onto the floor and feed him something as the wall goes down. That should do the trick – he'll look as though he's just munched us.'

'Brilliant!' said Jake.

So they waited patiently for Professor Niblett and about an hour later, as the wall began to move, Harry leapt into action.

'Jake, go and wait by the wall,' he said. He called Ron and fed him some leftover bits of sausage, then with super soccer speed he dashed over and waited with Jake.

The plan worked like a dream.

'Good morning, good morning, little . . . Oh, I see you've escaped from your prison,' said Professor Niblett.

Then he saw Ron eating the last bit of sausage. 'Eeek!' he shrieked. 'Get away from here, you dirty thing. Shoo!'

Ron, startled, darted off into the lab.

'What's this?' The Professor saw the empty beaker and then bent down to examine the mess on the floor. 'Eeewww! Not a nice way to go – eaten by rats. Oh well,' he said, standing up and brushing off his clothes, 'one less thing for me to worry about.'

He wondered if they had told anyone where they were going, but guessed they probably hadn't. He picked up the backpack. 'I'll just dump this in the dustbin on my way out.'

While Professor Niblett was in his secret museum, amusing himself with Harry and Jake's grisly end, they were in the lab looking for the shrinking device.

'Look,' said Harry pointing to the bench. 'There it is!'

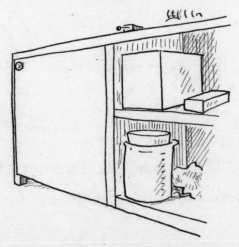

He set his Utility Boots to *Hover*, Jake jumped on for a piggyback, and then they rose up to the bench.

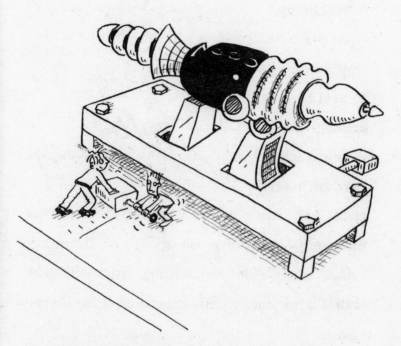

'Help me push it under the laser gun stand,' he said.

The shrinking device was heavy but they managed to push it underneath, where it would be hidden from the Professor. Then they hid there with it.

Soon they heard the wall slide shut and the Professor started searching for the shrinking device.

'Where did
I put the
stupid thing?'
he said to
himself. 'I'm
sure it was
here last night.'

He bent down and looked under the benches in case it had fallen on the floor. 'Dammit, where is it?!' He was getting frustrated. 'Oh well, I'll just have to find it before I leave for the station.'

I wonder what he's planning to do today, thought Harry. The thought was unsettling but he wasn't quite sure why.

They heard the front door close and then the crunching of gravel as Professor Niblett's car drove away.

'Good, he's gone,' said Jake. 'Let's get ourselves back to normal.'

'You'd better go first. I don't know if you'll be strong enough to push the lever when you're mini, but I can use my super soccer strength,' Harry said.

'Fair enough,' said Jake, only a little worried about being a guinea pig.

They dragged the shrinking device out and heaved it into the slot on the laser ray gun. Then Harry used his Utility Boots to take Jake over to the plinth opposite. He returned to the laser gun and got in position.

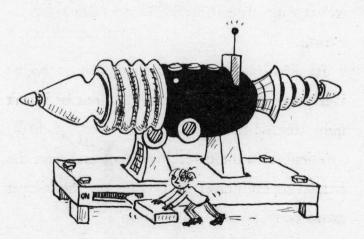

'Get ready, Jake,' said Harry, 'and keep your eyes closed!'

He put his shoulder to the lever and turned his Utility Boots to maximum jet force. Just as the boots were beginning to run out of power, the lever moved forward slowly. Then it slid in with a loud click and the laser beam shot straight at Jake.

At first Harry was worried that it wasn't working but then, through the haze of bright light, he could see that Jake was gradually growing. When he reached his usual size, the beam abruptly switched off and the lever returned to its original position.

And there was Jake, back to normal.

'My turn!' said Harry.

'Well, this is weird!' Jake said, carrying Harry
in his hand over to the plinth.

'How do you feel?' Harry asked.

Jake tried hard not to laugh at Harry's
squeaky voice. 'Absolutely fine,' he said.

He put Harry down, went back to the laser gun and pushed the lever forward. A few minutes later, Harry too was back to normal and they both breathed a huge sigh of relief. So did Ron.

Harry picked Ron up and gave him a hug.

'Right! Let's find out what that thief is planning!' he said, and dashed upstairs.

Chapter Eleven

Things Look Up

At the museum, Professor Niblett was making the final arrangements for his trip.

'Yes, that's right. I'm confirming my attendance at the museum conference in London. I also want to make sure that you have my ticket for the curators' Crown Jewel meeting. It will be ready for me at the hotel? That's wonderful, thank you for your help. I look forward to seeing you at the conference.'

The Professor clapped his hands together happily. 'I can't wait!!' he said.

Back at the house, Harry and Jake were in the kitchen. Professor Niblett had been making notes about his plan at the dinner table and had left the notebook open. Harry started to read and his face filled with horror.

'What is it, Harry?' said Jake. 'You look as though you just missed a penalty in the World Cup Final.'

'Look!' Harry handed the notebook to Jake.

Things to do

Get rid of kids (shrink to nothingness)
Go to museum and arrange travel and tickets
Pack bags / shrinker
Crown jewel conference
SHRINK!
Bring home and add to collection

'I knew he'd be planning something.' Harry was distraught. 'Suppose he steals the other World Cup when it comes here! We *have* to stop him from taking all these things. This is a job for Super Soccer Boy!'

'I know I always say this,' said Jake, 'but we could just call the police and let them handle it. I expect they're still at the museum anyway.'

'Oh yeah,' said Harry. 'Tell them that the Professor is using a shrinking ray to steal things from museums for his secret collection – and that he shrank us but now we're back to normal.

Somehow, I don't think they'd buy it.'

'Fair point, I guess,' said Jake. 'Well, we know he's coming back here to get the shrinker.'

'Yes,' said Harry. 'We must make sure he doesn't get his hands on it.'

'Well, that shouldn't be too difficult. We'll just hide it.'

'Hmm, the hard part will be making him confess,' said Harry.

'Yeah, like he's going to do that,' laughed Jake.

'We have to find a way to persuade him, or ...'

'Or what?'

'... scare him into it. I wonder – maybe we could use Ron!' Jake thought his friend had finally gone nuts.

'But Ron's a rat!'

'Duh . . . I'm aware of that. Come on, back to the lab.'

He grabbed Ron and dragged Jake downstairs, then ran over and put him on the plinth.

'Oh, I seeeee!' said Jake, suddenly twigging what Harry was up to.

'If the laser ray grows things that have been shrunk, maybe it can make full size things even bigger! I hope this works,' said Harry. 'One, two, three, GO!' He pushed the lever.

The laser beam lit up and Ron looked like a rat caught in headlights! Bit by bit he began to grow. Bigger and bigger.

'Harry, maybe you'd better turn it off!'

'Can't!' said Harry. 'It must be preset.'

'But he's getting REALLY big! I mean, how are we going to get him out of the basement?'

CRUNCH!!!

'Er, I think Ron's found a way,' said Harry.

Ron's head burst through the floor of the

kitchen above, sending the chairs and table flying in all directions. Just as it did, the beam shut off.

'BLIMEY!' said Harry.

'AWESOME!' said Jake.

They stood and gazed open mouthed at giant Ron.

'Come on, Ron!'

Ron burst through the remains of the kitchen window and stood outside, blinking.

Harry and Jake looked up at the five metre tall rat.

'Scary enough, do you think?' asked Harry.

Chapter Twelve

Ratzilla

Meanwhile, Professor Niblett was cheerfully trundling his way home in his Smart car.

Back at the house, Harry and Jake lay in wait with giant Ron.

'So you know the plan,' said Harry.

'Yep. You get him to confess, I record him on my phone and play it back to the police,' said Jake.

'That's it, and we'll wait for them to arrest him down in the basement, so they can see the mask and all of the things he's stolen.'

Unaware of what was about to happen, Professor Niblett turned into the driveway of his house. He drove up to the front door, stopped the car and hopped out chirpily.

'Welcome home, Professor,' said Harry, stepping out from the bushes.

'What?!' exclaimed the Professor, swinging round to look at Harry. 'But I thought . . .' He looked beyond Harry and froze instantly. 'I . . . I . . . I . . .'

'You thought Ron had eaten us? Yes, I know. How about if he ate you instead?'

Harry tugged at Ron's fur and he stood up on his back legs, towering menacingly over Professor Niblett.

'Get it away from me,' he squealed, terrified.

'Not until you confess!' said Harry. 'And promise to give back everything you've stolen.'

'Never! Not my pretty things. I shan't.' He turned and ran.

'Ron, fetch!' shouted Harry.

Ron went after the Professor and stopped him with a big heavy paw. Then he picked him up and took him back to Harry.

The Professor was shaking with fear.

'Confess,' demanded Harry, 'or I'll tell him to gobble you up.' He winked at Jake.

'No!' screamed the Professor as he looked at Ron's big scary teeth. 'No!!'

'This is your last chance, Professor.'

Ron's big pink tongue flicked out of his mouth and licked the Professor's face. He was just being friendly, but the Professor didn't know that.

'Aaaaaargh!' he screeched. 'OK, I confess, I CONFESS!! It was me who stole the funeral mask,' he wailed.

'And what about the other stuff in your basement?'

'Yes, and I stole all the other precious things from other museums too.'

Harry smiled.

'Did you get that, Jake?'

Jake nodded.

'OK, Ron, put him down.'

Ron gently placed the Professor on the ground and began to clean his whiskers.

'OK, Jake, call the police. Professor if you'd

like to lead me down to the basement, we'll wait for the police in your secret museum.'

Harry got out the shrinking device and pointed it at Ron and in a flash, Ron shrank back to normal. Harry picked him up and followed the Professor down to the basement. He watched as the wall panel descended into the floor.

'You know, Professor, you could have used your shrinking ray to do much more useful things than stealing,' Harry said, looking at the treasures in the secret room.

He gazed once again at the World Cup trophy and couldn't resist getting out his phone to take a picture. Absent-mindedly, he put the shrinker down on the table.

Suddenly, the Professor realised he had one last chance. He darted over and grabbed the ray.

'Aha! Now I've got you!' he said. 'And when I've shrunk you to nothing, I'll shrink everything else so the police can't find it! Mwahahahaha!'

He pointed the shrinker at Harry, but Harry's super soccer speed meant that he was too fast for him. Harry dodged out of the way and all the Professor succeeded in shrinking was a pile of books and a very surprised looking spider.

'Drat!' said the Professor, aiming again and again, but Harry was simply too fast.

Then, disaster! The Professor shrank the plinth just as Harry was vaulting over it, and Harry went flying. He grabbed at the bench as he fell, pulling off the shiny case that had held the laser ray gun.

'I've got you now!' chuckled the Professor looking at Harry sprawled on the floor. He aimed once more.

Harry quickly held up the box to shield himself and the ray was reflected into the secret museum.

'Oh no!' said Harry, as he watched the World Cup trophy shrink before his eyes.

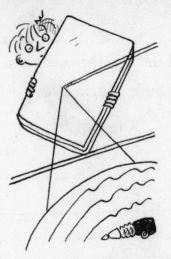

The Professor aimed again, and again Harry shielded himself with the shiny box. This time however, the beam hit the laser ray gun, shrinking it so it looked like a child's toy.

'Drat!' said the Professor. 'I'll get you for this!'

But Harry was on his feet again, darting towards him, dodging the laser blasts like a striker dodging defenders on a pitch. As he aimed once more, Harry, with a

flying scissor kick, knocked the shrinker out of
the Professor's hand. They both watched as it
flew through the air.

BOO OF

It landed hard on the floor. Before it finally shattered into pieces, it went off one more time. Harry watched in horror as the Jules Rimet trophy got the final blast and shrank away to nothing. He couldn't believe it.

Chapter Twelve

Cup Final Analysis

Moments later, the basement was full of police.

As they led the Professor away, babbling about shrinking and enlarging rays and giant rats, away Harry was still crawling around on the floor searching for the lost trophy.

'Looks like it's really gone this time,' said Jake sadly.

'Yes, it does,' sniffed Harry. 'Even with my super soccer vision I can't see it.'

'OK, lads,' said Inspector Bird. 'Thank you for your help, but we really need to get the crime team in. We'll get your statements later.'

'Of course, Inspector,' said Harry, and he and Jake went upstairs.

They walked down the driveway of Niblett Mansion.

'No one will ever know what really happened to the Jules Rimet cup,' said Jake. 'No one would ever believe us if we told them.'

'True,' agreed Harry, but he was smiling. 'We'll never forget it though,' he added, showing Jake the picture of the World Cup he'd taken with his phone.

'Awesome!' said Jake.

HARRY'S FOOTBALL FACTS!

In 1998 Macclesfield mascot, Roary the Lion, was sent off during a match against Lincoln City.

Ivory Coast striker Didier Drogba has a beer and a brand of chocolate named after him

DIDIER BEER

DROGBA CHOC

In the 1950's Lincoln City had a centre half named Ray LONG who was over 6 feet tall, and a left winger called David SHORT who was only 5 foot 4 inches.

Scottish goalkeeper Andy Goram has won three cricket caps for Scotland.

In winter 1963 Halifax Town FC opened up its frozen ground to be used as an ice rink!

The highest football stadium in the world is in Cerro de Pasco, in Peru. Players hate to play there because of the lack of oxygen!

In Saudi Arabia, the Education Ministry postponed school exams so that children could watch the World Cup.

In a West Ham match in 1970, Bobby Moore knocked out the referee with an attempted clearance.

Join
Super Soccer Boy
online:

www.supersoccerboy.com

⚽ Fun activities
⚽ Football facts and quiz
⚽ All the latest
on the books
⚽ And much more!